A message to naughty bunnies
everywhere: **BEHAVE!**
— P. A.

For the baddest bunny on the block
– Theo Benjamin Wreford-Bush
— B. M.

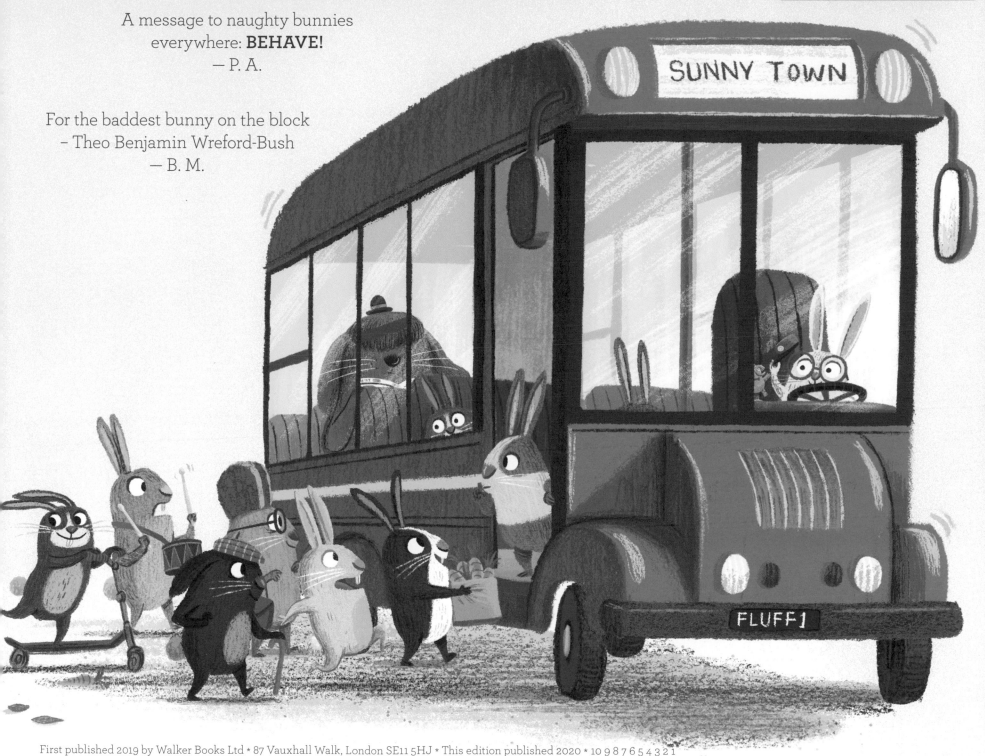

First published 2019 by Walker Books Ltd * 87 Vauxhall Walk, London SE11 5HJ * This edition published 2020 * 10 9 8 7 6 5 4 3 2 1
Text © 2019 Philip Ardagh * Illustrations © 2019 Ben Mantle * The right of Philip Ardagh and Ben Mantle to be identified as the author and illustrator respectively of this work
has been asserted by them in accordance with the Copyright, Designs and Patents Act 1988 * This book has been typeset in Archer Book * Printed in China * All rights reserved.
No part of this book may be reproduced, transmitted or stored in an information retrieval system in any form or by any means, graphic, electronic or mechanical, including
photocopying, taping and recording, without prior written permission from the publisher * British Library Cataloguing in Publication Data: a catalogue record for this book is
available from the British Library * ISBN 978-1-4063-9401-6 * www.walker.co.uk

There's a turtle at a bus-stop,
waiting with her shopping.
A bus whizzes past her
with no sign of stopping.

Bunnies on the bus!
Bunnies on the bus!

No wonder there's a fuss
about the bunnies on the bus!

Little Bunny at the wheel!
Little Bunny at the wheel!

He's swerving round the corners
to make the others SQUEAL!

Pandas at the crossing!
Pandas at the crossing!

ZOOOOOOOOOOOOM!

Their shopping jumping in the air,
spinning and a' tossing.

Bunnies on the bus!
Bunnies on the bus!

No wonder there's a fuss
about the bunnies on the bus!

Baby Bunny wails!
Baby Bunny wails!

Mummy Bunny
SOOTHES him

by reading Bunny Tales.

GOLDIFLOPS
and the THREE
BEARS

Lambs by the library,
playing on the swings.
The bus goes shooting past them,
flying without wings!

Bunnies in the aisle! Bunnies in the aisle!

DO sit down,
or you'll end up in a pile!

There's a bunny on the roof! THERE'S A BUNNY ON THE ROOF!

Watch out, you silly bunny! You may well lose a tooth!

Bunnies on the bus!
Bunnies on the bus!

No wonder there's a fuss
about the bunnies on the bus!

Bunnies at the stop!
Bunnies at the stop!

Time to get off now.

They jump down with a HOP!

But wait.

What's happening down in Station Lane?

The bunnies from the bus
have jumped onto a ...

TRAIN!

Bunnies on the train!
Bunnies on the train!

Another bunny journey...

Here we go again!